The A to Z Beastly Jamboree

S0-BNU-914

The A to Z Beastly Jamboree

Robert Bender

PUFFIN BOOKS

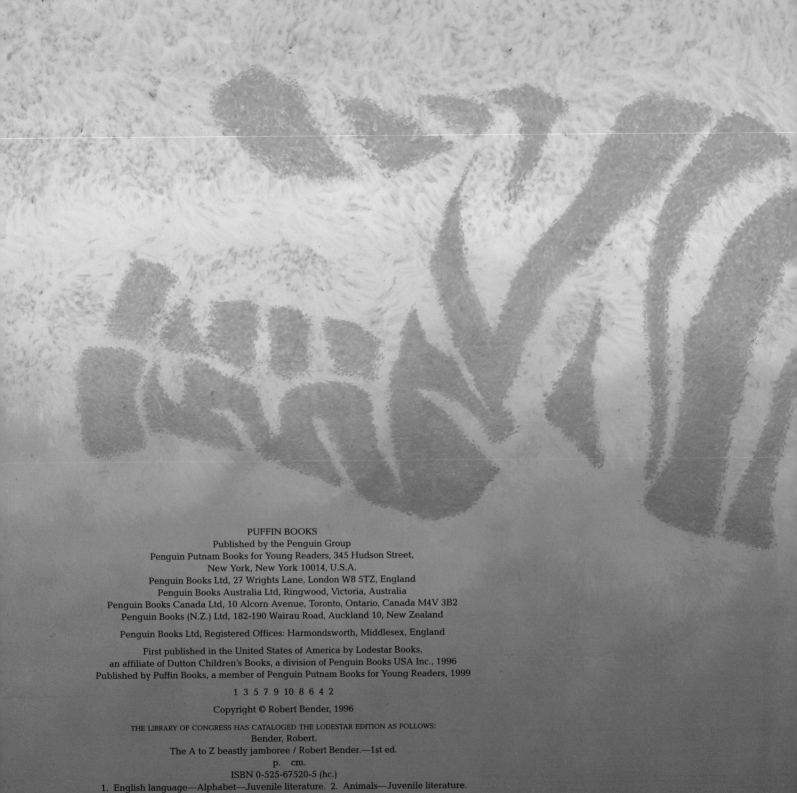

PUFFIN BOOKS
Published by the Penguin Group
Penguin Putnam Books for Young Readers, 345 Hudson Street,
New York, New York 10014, U.S.A.
Penguin Books Ltd, 27 Wrights Lane, London W8 5TZ, England
Penguin Books Australia Ltd, Ringwood, Victoria, Australia
Penguin Books Canada Ltd, 10 Alcorn Avenue, Toronto, Ontario, Canada M4V 3B2
Penguin Books (N.Z.) Ltd, 182-190 Wairau Road, Auckland 10, New Zealand

Penguin Books Ltd, Registered Offices: Harmondsworth, Middlesex, England

First published in the United States of America by Lodestar Books,
an affiliate of Dutton Children's Books, a division of Penguin Books USA Inc., 1996
Published by Puffin Books, a member of Penguin Putnam Books for Young Readers, 1999

1 3 5 7 9 10 8 6 4 2

Copyright © Robert Bender, 1996

THE LIBRARY OF CONGRESS HAS CATALOGED THE LODESTAR EDITION AS FOLLOWS:
Bender, Robert.
The A to Z beastly jamboree / Robert Bender.—1st ed.
p.   cm.
ISBN 0-525-67520-5 (hc.)
1. English language—Alphabet—Juvenile literature. 2. Animals—Juvenile literature.
[1. Alphabet. 2. Animals. 3. English language—Verb.] I. Title.
PE1155.B395 1996 421'.1—dc20 [E] 94-37189 CIP AC

Puffin ISBN 0-14-056213-3

Printed in the United States of America

Except in the United States of America, this book is sold subject to the condition that it shall not,
by way of trade or otherwise, be lent, re-sold, hired out, or otherwise circulated without the pub-
lisher's prior consent in any form of binding or cover other than that in which it is published and
without a similar condition including this condition being imposed on the subsequent purchaser.

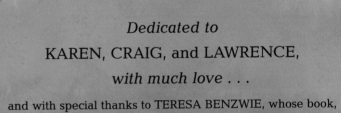

Dedicated to

KAREN, CRAIG, and LAWRENCE,

with much love . . .

and with special thanks to TERESA BENZWIE, whose book,
A Moving Experience (Zephyr Press), inspired this book

Ants anchor Aa

Bats boil **Bb**

Cows carry Cc

Dodos decorate **Dd**

Elephants embrace Ee

Frogs follow **Ff**

Goats guard **Gg**

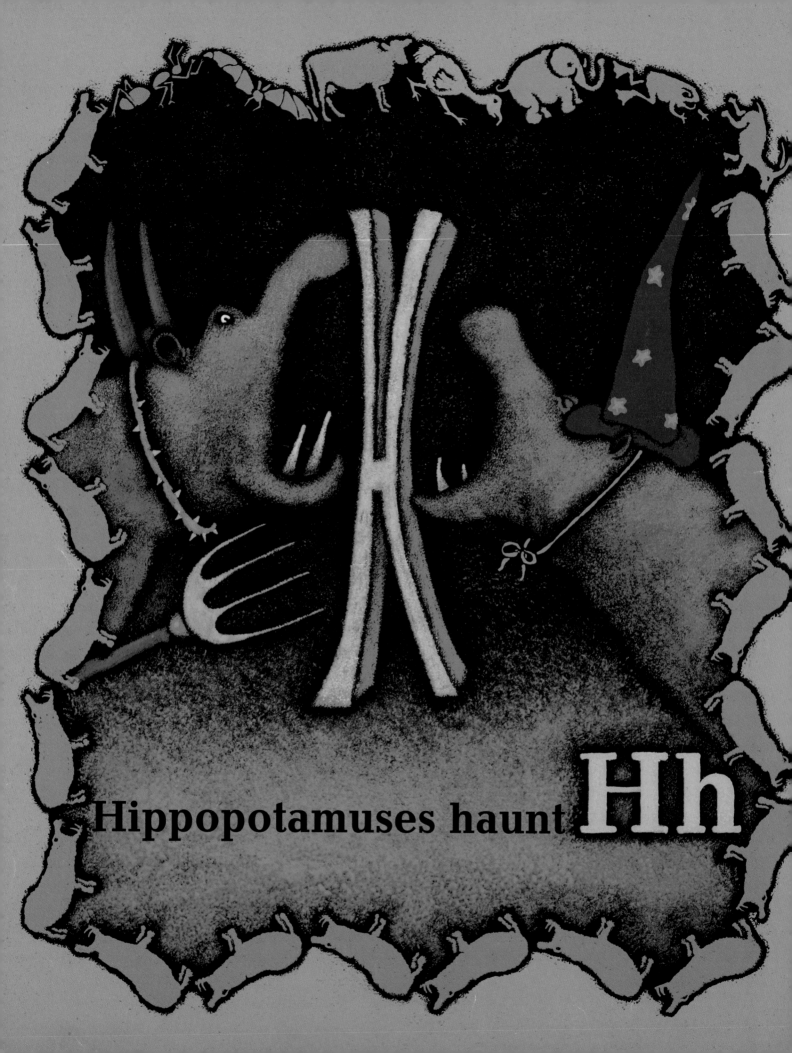

Hippopotamuses haunt **Hh**

Iguanas illuminate **Ii**

Jaguars jostle Jj

Kangaroos kiss **Kk**

Lions launch Ll

Mice mail **Mm**

Narwhals needle **Nn**

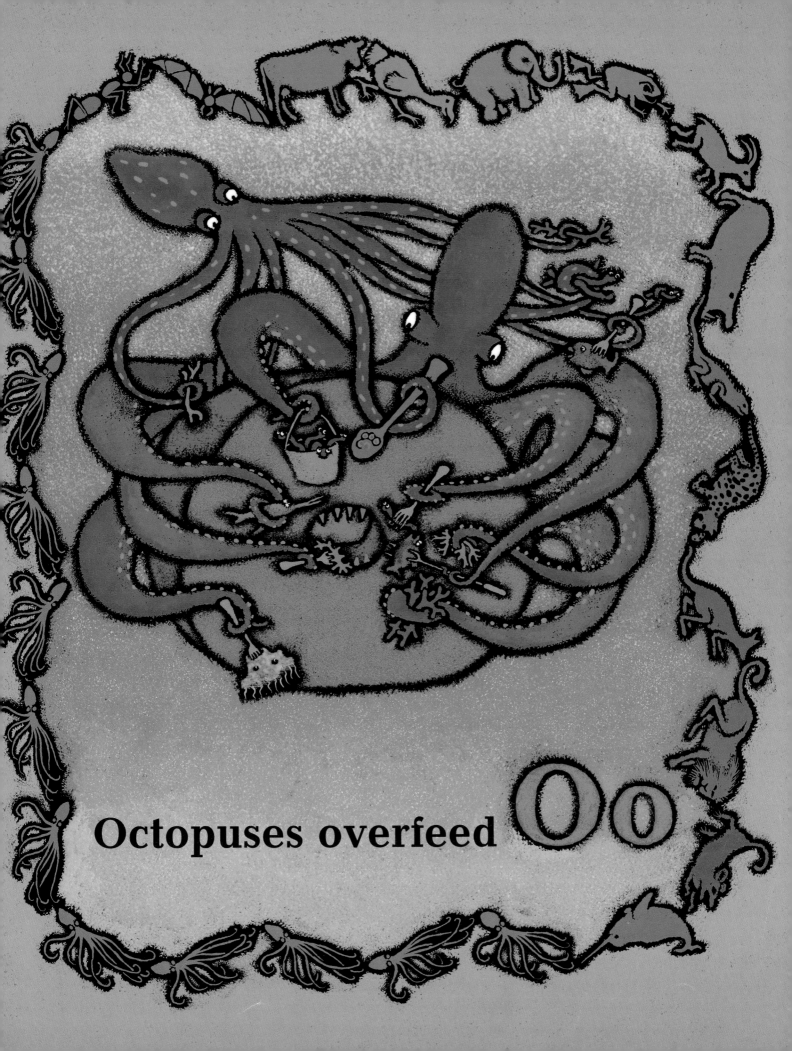

Octopuses overfeed Oo

Pigs purchase **Pp**

Quails quilt Qq

Rhinoceroses ruin Rr

Snakes saw **Ss**

Turtles tackle **Tt**

Unicorns undress **Uu**

Voles visit Vv

Walruses wrestle **Ww**

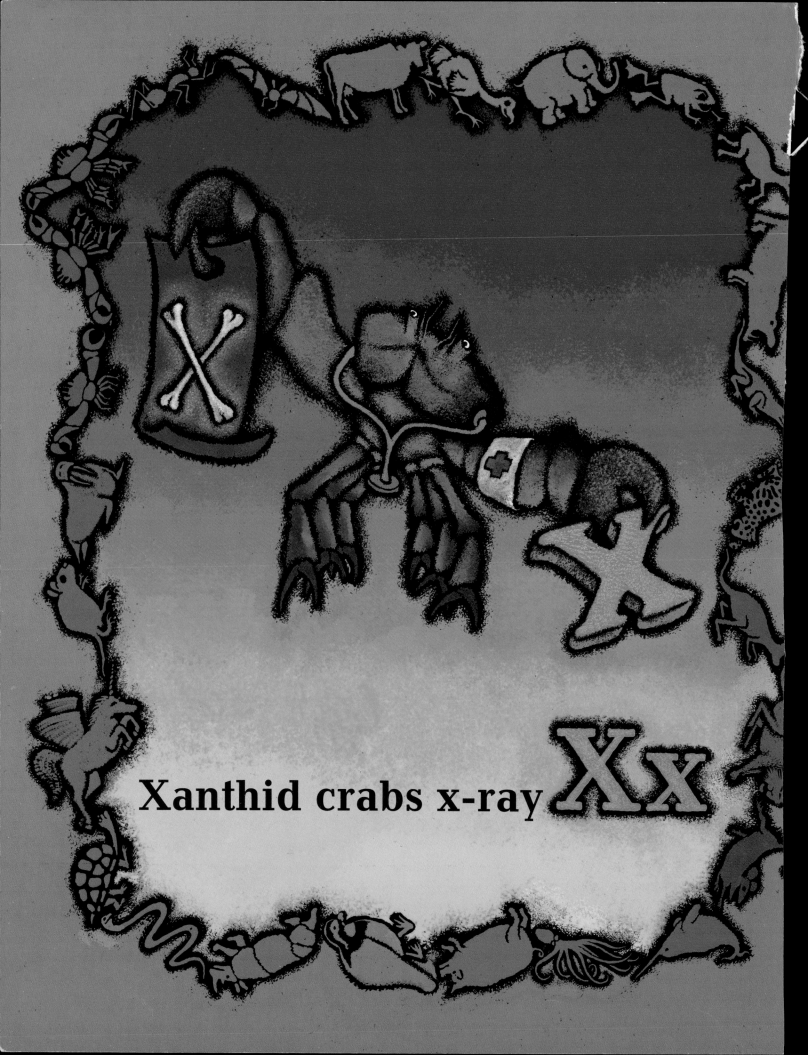

Xanthid crabs x-ray Xx

Yaks yank Yy

Zebras zipper Zz